Tea Party Rules

by **Ame Dyckman**

illustrated by **K. G. Campbell**

VIKING
An Imprint of Penguin Group (USA) Inc.

Cub was playing in the woods
when he smelled something delicious.
He followed his nose through the
bushes and found . . .

cookies!

And another bear.

"Can I have a cookie?"
Cub asked.
The bear just stared.

Cub tried again.
"Can I have a cookie, *please*?"
The bear just stared.

"Why won't you answer?" Cub cried.

He poked the bear.

The bear fell over.

"Oh!" Cub exclaimed. "*You* can't eat cookies!"

Cub felt sorry for the bear.

"I'll eat the cookies for you," he promised.

Cub was about to take a bite when
he heard someone coming.
He had no time to hide.

Cub pretended to be the other bear.

"It's time to play Tea Party!" the girl announced.

The girl paused.

She looked closely at Cub.

"You're grubby," the girl said.

"Tea Party Rule: you must be clean.

Then we can have cookies."

She carried Cub inside . . .

and put him in the tub.
Cub liked being grubby.
He did not want to be clean.

But he wanted cookies.

When Cub was clean, the girl paused again.
She looked very closely at Cub.

"You're messy," the girl said.
"Tea Party Rule: you must be neat.
Then we can have cookies."

She carried Cub to her room.

Cub liked being messy.
He did not want to be neat.

But he did want cookies.

When Cub was neat, the girl paused once more.
She looked very, *very* closely at Cub.

"Something is still not right," the girl said.
"Tea Party Rule: you must be fancy.
Then we can have cookies."

She pulled out her dress-up trunk.

Cub was certain he did not want to be fancy.
He wanted to run away.

But he **really** wanted cookies.

"Perfect!" the girl said.

"You're ready to play Tea Party!"

She carried Cub outside.
There were the cookies!

"Now," the girl said, "the most
important Tea Party Rule is . . .
you must eat *daintily*."

Cub couldn't believe it.
He was clean. He was neat.
He was wearing a dress!
And he had to eat daintily?

This was too much for a bear.
So Cub helped himself.

The girl gasped.
"YOU'RE NOT FOLLOWING THE RULES!" she shouted.

Cub did not care. *He* had cookies.

Soon only one cookie was left.

The girl sniffled. "I *really* wanted cookies," she said.
Cub knew how that felt. He gave the girl the last cookie.

But the girl did not eat daintily.
She said . . .

"We're not playing Tea Party anymore.
Now we're playing . . ."

"Bear!"

Cub liked this game much better than Tea Party.
And he already knew the Rules.

For Super Agent Scott,
who bears with me.
—A. D.

For Marianna,
a dear sister and snappy dresser.
—K. G.

VIKING
An imprint of Penguin Young Readers Group
Published by the Penguin Group
Penguin Group (USA) Inc.
375 Hudson Street
New York, New York 10014, U.S.A.

USA / Canada / UK / Ireland / Australia / New Zealand / India / South Africa / China
Penguin Books Ltd, Registered Offices: 80 Strand, London WC2R 0RL, England

For more information about the Penguin Group visit www.penguin.com

First published in the United States of America by Viking, an imprint of Penguin Young Readers Group, 2013

Text copyright © Ame Dyckman, 2013
Illustrations copyright © Keith Campbell, 2013

LIBRARY OF CONGRESS CATALOGING-IN-PUBLICATION DATA
Dyckman, Ame.
Tea party rules / by Ame Dyckman ; illustrated by K.G. Campbell.
pages cm
Summary: "A bossy little girl makes a bear cub follow all the rules at her tea party
before he is allowed to eat any of the cookies"— Provided by publisher.
ISBN 978-0-670-78501-8 (hardcover)
Special Markets ISBN 978-0-451-47010-2 Not For Resale
[1. Etiquette—Fiction. 2. Bears—Fiction. 3. Animals—Infancy—Fiction. 4. Tea—Fiction. 5. Parties—Fiction.]
I. Campbell, K. G. (Keith Gordon), date – illustrator. II. Title.
PZ7.D9715Te 2013
[E]—dc23   2012046989

Manufactured in China

3   5   7   9   10   8   6   4   2

Designed by Jim Hoover   Set in Horley Old Style MT Std
The illustrations for this book are rendered in sepia marker and colored pencil.

The publisher does not have any control over and does not assume
any responsibility for author or third-party websites or their content.

This Imagination Library edition is published by Penguin Young Readers, a division
of Penguin Random House, exclusively for Dolly Parton's Imagination Library,
a not-for-profit program designed to inspire a love of reading and learning, sponsored
in part by The Dollywood Foundation. Penguin's trade editions of this work are
available wherever books are sold.